There's a Monster IN YOUR BOOK

Written by TOM FLETCHER

Illustrated by GREG ABBOTT

Random House 🏠 New York

For Miss Summer Rae, the newest monster in the family! —T.F.

For Roger —G.A.

Visit us on the Web! randomhousekids.com

Educators and librarians, for a variety of teaching tools, visit us at RHTeachersLibrarians.com

Library of Congress Cataloging-in-Publication Data is available upon request.

ISBN 978-1-5247-6456-2 (trade) — ISBN 978-1-5247-6457-9 (ebook)

MANUFACTURED IN CHINA
10 9 8 7 6 5 4 3
First American Edition

OH NO!
There's a monster in your book!

Let's try to get him out.

shake the book
and turn the page....

Nice try—that knocked him over, but he's
STILL IN YOUR BOOK!

Tickle

his feet and turn the page. . . .

That didn't work—he's just laughing and he's
STILL IN YOUR BOOK!

Try blowing him away.

BLOOW

really hard and turn the page. . . .

That's better—now he's far away. But he's
STILL IN YOUR BOOK!

TILT the book to the left. . . .

Now he's over here, but he's
STILL IN YOUR BOOK!

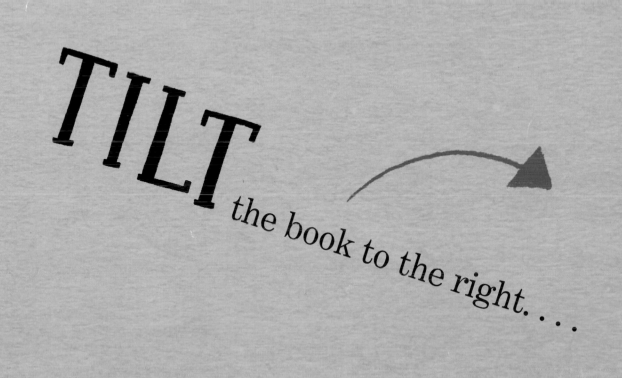

TILT the book to the right....

He's hanging on!

What a naughty little monster!

Give the book a good

Wiggle....

Good, now he's back over there.
But there's **STILL** a monster in your book!

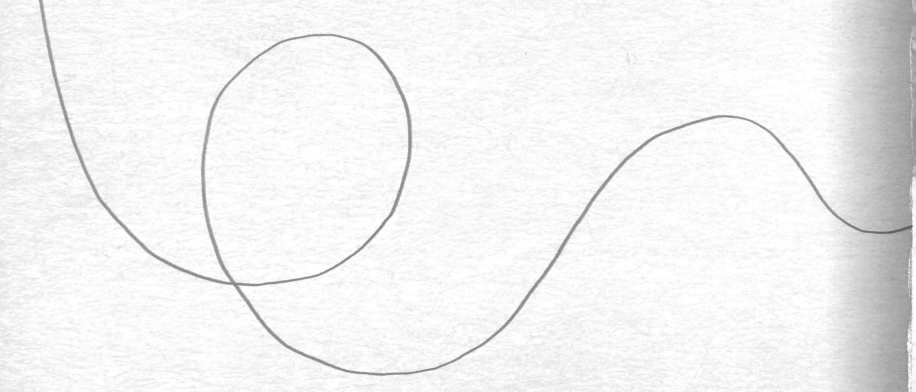

Try **spinning** the book around and around. . . .

Look! He's dizzy!

Quick, make a

LOUD

noise. . . .

It's working! He's running away!

Make that noise again, but . . .

HE'S GONE!

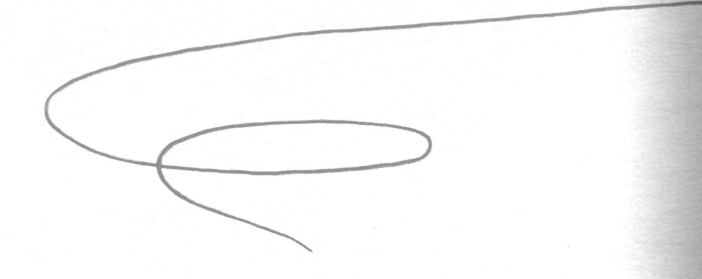

There **ISN'T** a monster in your book anymore....

Now he's in your room!

Quickly, call him back!
Monster, come back!

Look! Here he is!
He's coming back.

Keep calling him. . . .
Monster!
Come here, little Monster!

PHEW!

He's back in your book.

You don't want a monster loose in your room!
This book is probably the best place to keep him.

Monster, you can stay here in this book!

Pet Monster's head and say good night. . . .

Good night, Monster.

SHHH!
Look! He's fast asleep.

Gently close the book so he doesn't wake up.